Literally

CHRISTMAS

C. Streetlights

Editing by – Tiffany Fox; Beyond DEF
Cover design by – LeTeisha Newton; Beyond DEF
Book interior design by – Deena Rae; Beyond DEF, adaptation for ebook

For information contact:

Beyond DEF Publishing Services, LLC
info@beyonddeflit.com

ISBN - Print: 978-0-9984288-2-6
ISBN - eBook: 978-0-9984288-3-3

OTHER BOOKS

Tea and Madness
https://books2read.com/teaandmadness

Black Sheep, Rising
https://books2read.com/BlackSheepRising

CONTENTS

DEDICATION

For Mama—
I'll open a door to find you when it's time to use my key.

ACKNOWLEDGMENTS

I want to express my gratitude for my family and for their excitement over this book. As always, they are my biggest support system and I would not be able to find the motivation to write if it weren't for the three of them. Of course, I should not forget Frankie, my King Charles Cavalier, who supervises me in my office. She, too, supports me in her own way.

I also want to thank everyone involved with its publication at Beyond DEF Publishing, as they are the reason *Literally Christmas* exists in its current form in the first place. Thank you, Tiffany, LJ, Deena Rae, and LeTeisha. Your professionalism and knowledge improves my craft tremendously.

I must also thank my hair stylist, Janeen, who encourages my strange sense of whimsy and keeps me accountable by always asking me what I'm working on when I come in to get my hair done. Thank you for being an unknowing taskmaster I don't want to let down!

And lastly, thank you to my readers—you have all made the holiday season more magical. I hope you all find sweet baby hippos under your trees.

Literally CHRISTMAS

Dear Santa,

I don't know why I'm writing this. It's not like I've ever truly believed in the magic of Christmas, but what do I have to lose? My mother can't look at me, my father doesn't know whose side to take, and my sister is in total denial of everything. Life hasn't always been that great, you know? I never really felt like I fit in anywhere, and my parents always denied my sister and me the joys of any holiday, including Christmas and birthdays. Maybe — just maybe I want to try to believe. Yes, that's my Christmas wish.

Natalie St. Clair

Dear Natalie,
Be careful what you wish for.

Ho, ho, ho!
Santa

Literally

CHRISTMAS

PROLOGUE

The night was dark and clear, with only white flakes falling from the sky to indicate direction—if the flakes fell from top to bottom, one knew immediately which way was up and which way was down. There were no streetlights, no road signs, no stores or marketplaces to stand as a corner landmark to tell someone whether to turn right or left. There was only the snow reflecting the full moon, and countless snow-covered pine trees stood upright in fields surrounding at least one crystalline lake. If one were to look up, it would be impossible to distinguish stars from flakes until they landed upon one's forehead and cheeks, the burning sensation equal to both fire from a star and ice from a snowflake.

And then there was the silence.

The silence seemed unnatural except for the subtle sound of merriment carrying itself on the winter wind. Happy voices and cheerful laughter seasoned the crisp air like peppermint candy swirled into freshly made whipped cream. It didn't seem out of place, but it had to come from somewhere.

If one were to follow the voices on that certain night and peek inside a frosted window, one would find a party in a workshop. Tables that were once in the middle of the shop had been pushed to the sides of the room. People danced to the lively music played by a small band standing on a round table at the front of the room. Everyone wore their best green dresses and shorts with matching shirts, red-and-white striped tights were clean and straight, and the bakers had contributed delicious tarts and cookies.

Nobody would have noticed a small child, perhaps about four-years-old, toddle out from the nursery upstairs at all. But the small child noticed everything—from the paper streamers held in place by magic holly berries to the fiddlers on the table—and her wide eyes filled with candy canes that seemed to dance. She scurried along the side of the wall, avoiding dancers and revelers, and slipped into the next room.

Not one person saw her slip into the back seat of the gleaming red sleigh with gilded edges where she could still watch the adults in the workshop, filling her imagination with sights and sounds she would never forget.

While preparing the sleigh for its flight the next day, Christmas Eve, not one person thought to look underneath the furs in the back seat where she was sound asleep.

ONE

Natalie parked her car in front of a modest brick home and groaned. It was the second Monday of the month—time for her monthly breakfast with her parents. As usual, she was not looking forward to the ninety-minute appointment. But she couldn't very well stay hiding in her car, so she quickly checked herself in the mirror and stepped out into the brisk fall air.

The leaves fell from the trees, and Natalie noticed some neighbors had begun stringing up Christmas lights, something her parents would never do. She snorted. Sherry and Martin St. Clair had never decorated their home for any holiday nor had they ever permitted gifts. Natalie frowned and walked up to the door and rang the bell.

"You're late," Sherry said as she opened the door. "We thought you weren't coming."

Natalie stood there wondering if she would be permitted to enter. "I was stuck behind a train, Sherry. It's only five minutes."

Natalie had never called Sherry "Mom" or "Mother." From the time the St. Clairs had adopted and another little girl, they had insisted on being Sherry and Martin.

Sherry's mouth pressed into a thin line, making her lips disappear. "Very well, come in then." She stepped aside, allowing her to cross the threshold.

3

Natalie entered the house where she had grown up. There were no warm feelings, no rush of sentimentality that often comes over a person when walking into their family home. Only a sense of resolution. This would be her last obligatory meal with the St. Clairs.

Her sister had been fortunate to earn a full-ride scholarship to college. Once she graduated high school, she left the St. Clair home and never looked back. Chloe and Natalie regularly texted and emailed, but to Chloe, the St. Clairs didn't exist anymore.

Natalie hadn't been so lucky, however, and had to rely on Sherry and Martin to pay for her college tuition. Monthly breakfast began the month after graduation, and she had to bring a check to each appointment.

It all ended today.

Natalie followed Sherry into the dining room, unsurprised to see Martin already eating while reading the newspaper. The cherry dining table had the usual selection of fruit and croissants, but there were eggs and bacon too, which made Natalie suspicious. Sherry always attempted hospitality when they were about to do something especially out of character.

A strange expression crossed Sherry's face. "Sit down, Natalie, and have something to eat."

Natalie realized Sherry was attempting to smile. Something was definitely going on.

Martin folded his paper. "How is everything going with, uh, going with … what is it you do again?"

Natalie closed her eyes, not wanting to explain what event planning was again, but she did anyway to be polite.

"And that's going well?"

"It is. The company is doing well, and we're getting ready for the holiday rush." She put jam on her croissant and shut her mouth. Too much information would invite the trouble of more questions.

Sherry forced and twisted her face into a grimace-like smile. "Do you have plans for Thanksgiving, Natalie? We thought it would be so nice if you could join us because, uh …" She cleared her throat. "Well, uh, since you are our daugh—" She choked on her piece of fruit.

Natalie stared at her like she had grown another arm.

Martin reached over and patted Sherry's hand. "What your mother is trying to say …"

That was it. She was clearly in an alternate universe. Natalie stood and pulled her check from her purse. "I don't know what is going on here, or what you are up to, but this is like some weird *On Golden Pond* stuff, and I don't want anything to do with it. There's my money, just like we agreed. Thanks for breakfast and the show, but I'm done."

She was almost to the door when she heard them move, frantically following her and reaching her in the hallway.

"Natalie, wait," Martin said.

She stopped for a moment to put on her coat.

"Take your check back, Natalie."

She paused and turned around, her suspicion growing even more. "Why?"

He walked forward and shoved it in Natalie's hand and she awkwardly took it. "Just take it."

Natalie looked up at Sherry whose face had contorted into a strange, scrunched-up version of itself, red and splotchy. Bowing her head, she hid her eyes behind her hands. Was she crying? What was going on?

"I know we weren't good parents to you and Chloe," Martin started.

"What is this?" Natalie demanded.

"Just listen," Martin pleaded. Sherry's sniffles grew louder. "We weren't good parents. We made terrible mistakes."

"Mistakes?" Natalie yelled. "Are you talking about the time when all Chloe and I wanted was *one* birthday party and you *forgot* our birthdays?"

He looked away.

"Or how about the time Miss Gladys from across the street gave Chloe and me a Christmas present and you and Sherry put it away for us to open on Christmas and then lost it? Or the time I was in the second-grade play and everyone else's parents showed up except for mine, and my teacher, Mrs. Miller, had to sit in Sherry's reserved seat? Were those *all* mistakes?"

Sherry openly sobbed, but Natalie didn't care. These weren't "mistakes;" they were deliberate cruelties to a child.

"Natalie, we weren't perfect …" Martin began.

She threw her head back and laughed scornfully. "Chloe and I didn't need *perfection*, Martin. You took us from an orphanage.

All we needed was *love*. You couldn't even give us that. We couldn't even have a mom or a dad. All we got was a Sherry and a Martin!" Natalie looked at them, confused. "And now you want to explain?" She snorted. "No, you don't get to do that." She turned to the door and stepped outside, the crisp sunshine greeting her.

"Sherry is dying."

The door closed softly, even sadly, behind her.

TWO

Natalie looked up at the sky and sighed. Martin wasn't one for dramatics, so she knew it was true: Sherry was dying.

So now what?

She walked back to her car and, trying to feel guilty that she didn't spend the full ninety minutes with Martin and Sherry, started the drive back to her townhome.

Dialing Chloe's number and connecting her Bluetooth, she waited for her sister to answer.

"Wait, why are you up so early? Did they drop dead?" Her sister's cheerful voice filled her car.

"Chloe, my God—" Natalie snorted. "You either don't know, in which case, I have news, or you do know and you don't care."

"What are you talking about?"

"Have you talked to them? At all?"

"I don't talk to them. I won't. Martin has called every other day for the last two weeks, so I know they're alive."

Natalie drove through town, autumn reds and yellows flashing by outside her window, and debated telling Chloe herself or telling her to talk to Martin. Her sister's laugh made up her mind.

"How'd you escape breakfast so early, anyway?"

"I guess Sherry is dying, Chloe."

Silence.

"Chloe?"

"She's dying?" Chloe nearly whispered.

Natalie frowned. "Yeah, but I don't know anything else." She filled her sister in on Martin and Sherry's awkwardness that morning, including their attempt at calling them their daughters.

Chloe was suddenly angry. "Son of a– Ugh! Do they really think they can just apologize?"

"I know, Chloe." Natalie pulled into her garage and thought back to the late-night conversations they'd had about how they might react if this day had come. How might they feel if Martin and Sherry had somehow finally recognized the years of damage they had inflicted on their two adopted daughters?

"Would you forgive them, Nat?" Chloe had whispered years ago when they were teenagers.

"I don't know. I don't know if I can." Natalie stared at the ceiling of their shared bedroom. Could they be the better people and accept their apologies?

Martin and Sherry had never physically hurt them, nor had they ever said mean things to them. She and Chloe were provided for, but the absence of affection had stripped away, layer by layer, their belief in themselves and anything magical. Natalie wondered if this could ever be apologized for.

Chloe was silent. "I wouldn't. I'm going to leave here and never come back. They won't have a chance to apologize." She was determined, and Natalie believed her. Her sister never said things she didn't mean.

"Maybe if they apologize it'll mean ..." Natalie's voice trailed away.

"What?"

She sighed. "I just mean ... maybe if they're sorry, it'll show that we really are worth loving." Natalie angrily wiped at the tears in her eyes. Martin and Sherry weren't worth crying over.

With steely resolve, Chloe said, "We don't have to wait for their apology for that, Nat. We love each other, and that's worth everything."

Her sister's tears echoed through the car, bringing her back to the present. "There aren't take backs for something like this, Natalie." Her whisper bounced across the interior and hit her chest.

"I'm sorry, sis."

"Don't be. You're my only family."

Natalie's heart ached.

Natalie ignored the voicemail from Martin on her phone the next morning and instead focused on the sketchpad on her desk. She would call him back later that night once she got home. They were approaching the busiest time of year at work and she felt like a kindergartner attempting trigonometry.

How does someone who hates Christmas plan festive and joyous Christmas parties?

"This is literally the worst time of year ever," she groaned and leaned back in her chair.

Caroline walked up next to her. "Don't let Victoria hear you say that. She loves the holidays. This is her favorite time of year."

Victoria breezed into the office holding a fall wreath and cornucopia. "Don't let me hear what?"

"I just don't see why the holidays are such a big deal. I mean, the business makes a lot of money, so I get why it's a big deal for us. I just don't know why everyone gets so excited about it." She frowned, shading the corner of her sketchpad.

"Oh, someone's a Grinch!" Victoria laughed.

"I'm not a Grinch. I'm just realistic." Natalie shrugged. "Thanksgiving and Christmas are literally just normal days we've set aside to eat something different and hang decorations on a tree. It's just weird."

"Well, I hope you're putting more thought into the McIntoshes' Christmas party than just decorations on a tree. That's a huge account for us."

Natalie had hoped Victoria wouldn't ask about that, and she spun around on her chair to face her desktop again. Victoria stepped behind her and spotted her sketchpad.

She pointed at the drawing. "I see a table with a poinsettia in the center. Come see me in my office." Victoria turned on her stilettos and walked away, stopping at her office door to hang the wreath before entering.

Natalie dropped her head to her desk. "Great," she muttered.

Caroline sat at her desk. "You're not getting fired."

Keeping her head down, she mumbled, "How do you know?"

"Victoria doesn't fire people right away. She gives too many chances." She pushed up her cardigan sleeves and pulled out her sketchpad.

Natalie groaned again and pulled herself up from her desk. "Just because you're my best friend, doesn't mean you can be right all the time." Straightening her dress and adjusting her hair, Natalie tentatively knocked on Victoria's door.

"Come in, Natalie."

With its shelves filled with books on design, architecture, and floral arrangement, Victoria's office looked more like a private library than an office. She had an ornate desk she rarely used. At least, Natalie had never seen her sitting behind it. Instead, Victoria opted to sit on the oversized loveseat and wingback chairs that were arranged in front of the floor-to-ceiling windows. Natalie found her sitting in one of the wingbacks with blanket over her lap, gesturing for Natalie to sit in one of the chairs.

"Come have a seat, Natalie, and tell me why you hate Christmas."

THREE

Natalie slowly sat down and thought about what she should say to Victoria. The woman had an uncanny ability to detect dishonesty the moment it entered her vicinity, so Natalie couldn't just lie and say she loved Christmas.

Victoria patted her gray updo. She was of indeterminate age, and Natalie always thought Victoria would make a perfect fairy godmother. "How about you start with the truth? It'll be so much easier on both of us." She took off her glasses and gave Natalie her full attention.

So much for bending the truth. "It's not so much that I hate Christmas, Victoria."

Her boss raised an eyebrow.

She hurried on. "It's that my sister and I weren't raised … conventionally."

Victoria waited for more, and when Natalie didn't comply, she raised an eyebrow. "Please continue."

"Our adopted parents didn't believe in celebrating holidays or birthdays, not for any religious reasons, but because they didn't believe in observing them. I mean, I guess that's what they believed. Holidays were just sort of … forgotten." Quietly, she added, "Chloe and I were forgotten."

Perhaps it was the news of Sherry's impending death, or not knowing what to do with an out-of-place apology, but Natalie found herself telling Victoria everything about how she and Chloe were raised. Victoria listened to Natalie's experiences and didn't interrupt. She only got up once to retrieve the tissue box from her desk when Natalie's tears threatened to fall.

"I suppose I don't understand Christmas. It's supposed to be this joyful and magical time, but it was always miserable for us. School was the only place we felt normal, but we didn't have school at Christmas because it was on break for two weeks. We were left on our own in a house where we were ignored. We only had each other."

"Well, you certainly have had a lot on your heart and chest for many years, Natalie. I'm glad you let all this go. Now, what to do about this?" Victoria tapped a finger against her lips, her brows knitting together contemplatively.

"I'm sorry?"

"We can't have you going around not understanding Christmas, especially when we're in the business of celebrating the holidays, can we? You're pathetic little poinsettia is not going to cut it around here. We need festive! And trees! And reindeer! And, of course, we need to lighten your heart a little bit along the way." Victoria chuckled.

Natalie was confused. "Um, so what do you have in mind?"

Victoria's bright-blue eyes twinkled with delight as she patted her hair again to make sure nothing was out of place.

"Why, we're going to have you work with Santa Claus, of course!"

Panic swelled in Natalie's chest, and her heartbeat thundered in her ears. "I'm sorry, but … *what?*"

"The best way for you to understand the spirit of Christmas is by working directly with the Father of the Holidays! Lucky for you, my brother-in-law is Santa Claus." Victoria's eyes beamed and her smile lit up the office.

"I'm sorry, b-but what?" Natalie repeated, unable to grasp Victoria's sudden excitement.

Victoria smiled patiently. "My brother-in-law is bringing his assistant with him next week so they can begin building his Enchanted Forest at Northpointe Mall. I help him set it up every year, and this year you will join me. After it is completed, you will be one of his elves and learn to love Christmas." She clapped her hands, thoroughly delighted.

Natalie fought the urge to vomit at the thought of mall decorations surrounding her along with fake snow and carols piped in to mock her misery. Worse, there would be children.

"Victoria, is this really necessary? I mean, can't I just study some magazines or look at some online portfolios?"

"You did that in school and you gave me a poinsettia on a table."

"But what about my work here? I can't expect Caroline to do everything while I'm playing elf," Natalie practically begged.

"Nonsense. You will work as an elf in the afternoon and evening, and you will work here in the morning. Santa won't expect you until after lunch, anyway."

Her shoulders slumped in defeat. Once Victoria made a decision, there was no dissuading her. "Thank you for this opportunity, Victoria," she mumbled.

"Of course, Natalie. We will build the Forest starting next week! Wear clothes that can get dirty." Victoria picked up her phone to make a call, and Natalie took the hint to leave.

She groaned inwardly and walked back to her desk, dramatically burying her head in her arms.

Caroline didn't even look up from her work. "I told you. You're not fired."

Natalie flipped off her friend and went back to burying her head.

"How bad could it possibly be?"

"It's so bad."

Caroline put her pencil down, walked over to her friend, and sat on the desk. "Come on, Nat, tell me," she urged, stroking Natalie's hair.

"I have to be an elf for Santa."

She froze. "I'm sorry, but what?"

FOUR

T he mall had been closed for an hour. Natalie had watched the last of the employees filter out of the side doors for the last fifteen minutes before she finally had enough courage to meet Victoria and her brother-in-law inside. Northpointe Mall hosted Santa every year, and Santa was found in his Enchanted Forest, but obviously, Natalie had never seen him as a child. Victoria had explained that her brother-in-law volunteered his time and services to Northpointe every year and had been doing this for as long as she'd known him, which seemed like a while, considering how ... *seasoned* Victoria was.

Victoria greeted her, eyes sparkling as usual, and welcomed Natalie with a warm hug. She hurried her inside and took her coat. "You're just in time. We just started opening the crates."

Taking in Victoria's denim overalls, penny loafers, and her silver-gray hair in the usual French knot at the top of her head, Natalie was suddenly self-conscious in her ripped jeans and paint-stained sweatshirt. "Am I dressed okay?"

"Of course, dear," Victoria patted her hand. "Now, let's get to work." She handed her a crowbar and walked over to a young man about Natalie's age. He laughed, and his face lit up with natural good humor.

"This is Mason, dear, Santa's assistant. He comes with my brother-in-law every year, and we are so lucky he does. Mason, this is Santa's helper this year. She's my employee, so be good to her." Victoria smiled.

"Of course! Hi, Natalie, welcome to Santa's Enchanted Forest." He motioned around him.

Natalie's eyebrows came together, and she leaned into him and pointed at his chest. "How did you know my name? Victoria didn't tell you my name."

Mason looked uncomfortable, more than likely because her finger was drilling a hole into breastbone. "Uh, Victoria told us about you before you got here. Sorry?" He backed away and straightened his sweater. "Would you rather I call you something else?"

She groaned, feeling ridiculous. "No, Nat is fine. I'm sorry, you probably think I'm a lunatic—"

"Maybe?"

"I'm just feeling a little out of my element with," she gestured to everything around her, "all of this."

"I get it. It must be a little like walking into a freak show right now after a life of not liking Christmas." He laughed but stopped suddenly, looking at her with alarm.

"How …?"

Backing away slowly and out of arm's reach, Mason stammered, "I-I'm going to go tell Santa you're here."

Still holding the crowbar, Natalie stood in the middle of a sea of crates and boxes and wondered at the chaos around her. It seemed everyone knew everything about her, poised and polished Victoria was prying lids off wooden crates, and everyone called the boss Santa. This was literally the most bizarre experience of her life.

A voiced boomed behind her. "Ho, ho, ho! This is Natalie!"

Natalie turned around and came face to face with Santa Claus. Of course, it wasn't the *real* Santa Claus—that would be farcical. This man was elfin, with his rosy cheeks and delight-filled blue eyes. His balding head was graced with cotton-like white hair that swirled the circumference as if playing a game of Ring-Around-A-Rosy. And his beard! His beard was downy white, resting below the clavicle in a perfect swoop from one ear to the next. It wasn't polite to comment on a person's weight, she knew, but it did appear the man before her had enjoyed a few cookies in his lifetime. If he were wearing St. Nick's red velvet suit with fur cuffs and hat, Natalie would have to question everything she'd ever thought false in her life, for surely, they were real. But this man simply wore jeans and a flannel.

No, *this* was actually the most bizarre experience of her life.

"I, uh, I, hi, yes, I'm Natalie, Mr. …?" Natalie didn't know what to say.

"Everyone calls me Santa." He laughed another genuine laugh clear from his belly to the backs of his eyes.

"Oh! Um, okay, Santa." The man was bonkerballs. "It's nice to meet you."

"My sister-in-law says you're in need of some Christmas spirit!" The man spoke heartily; there was no doubting his charisma.

His neighbors probably all think he's a nice guy. Natalie stopped herself. She was thinking of Santa like he was a serial killer. What was wrong with her?

"Yes! Yes, I think I do need Christmas spirit, Santa." A little Christmas Spirit wouldn't, well … kill her.

Caroline and Chloe exchanged knowing glances at breakfast the next morning while Natalie attempted to avoid their gazes. Finally, Caroline broke the silence. "So … how did it go last night?"

Natalie slowly buttered her toast knowing Caroline and Chloe were waiting for her response. She deliberately chose her words. "It was fine. I waited until everyone left the mall and Victoria let me in. Did you know Victoria's idea of dressing to build stuff is overalls and penny loafers? I mean, she was adorable, but I felt like a slob next to her."

"I don't think that's what Caroline meant, Natalie." Chloe narrowed her eyes. She always knew when Natalie wasn't telling the whole truth.

She sighed. "It was weird, okay?" She threw her toast onto her plate and took a sip of her mocha. "It's like I'm an elf caterpillar suffocating in a Christmas cocoon. And there's a guy there … Mason? He has hair and eyes and freckles and was wearing a button-down shirt that made his eyes look sparkly and his freckles look freckly, and …" Natalie raised a brow at their pointed looks and cleared her throat. "Well, Mason seems like he can do nothing wrong. He just touches a crate and it not only opens, but everything inside will just come together in no time. I swear, he's magical or something. I watched him open a crate with Santa's shop inside, and then I turned to ask Victoria something. When I turned back to help Mason build this thing, it was already done. I don't know how he did it, but there's something weird there."

The girls looked at each other, and Chloe leaned forward. "Okay, take a deep breath. You need to slow down, Natalie. We don't know what you're talking about right now."

Caroline shrugged. "You sound deranged."

Chloe snorted.

"Well, she does." She shrugged and finished chewing. "Sparkling eyes and freckly freckles? Touching crates and things that build themselves? What are you even talking about? The last thing you said that made any sense was Victoria was wearing penny loafers."

Natalie glared at her. "I stayed awake all night last night trying to figure it out, and I don't know how Mason could work so fast."

"Maybe he's an elf," Caroline offered dismissively.

"You haven't said anything about Santa," Chloe said.

Natalie went quiet. Why hadn't she mentioned Santa? Between his jolly shouts of "ho, ho, ho" and the genuine kindness, Natalie didn't know what she could say about him. She felt protective of him though. "Santa is just what you'd think him to be," she finally said.

Chloe stared at her hard. "A con man trying to sell a lie to little children? Cool."

"No. Think of every Santa image you've ever imagined: red cheeks, bright eyes, white beard, big belly, and generosity. That's the man I met last night."

"Take her temperature, Caroline, she's got a fever."

Caroline held her cup and tapped it with her fingers. "Maybe … maybe … this is the *real* Santa, Nat. He's come to teach you about Christmas."

Natalie snorted. "Sure. Santa Claus is working at Northpointe Mall."

Caroline threw part of her muffin at Natalie. "I'm serious. Maybe you should start believing in Christmas miracles."

Chloe rolled her eyes. "Or maybe you've lost your mind and the man is just committed to his seasonal job. At least Mason sounds cute."

Natalie shrugged. "I guess. For a miracle crate opener and builder."

"You 'guess.' You seem pretty flustered by him, Nat," Chloe teased. "Just enjoy what you can from the experience. It'll be over before you know it. Besides, how bad can it be?" She became serious and set her coffee cup on the table. "So I called Martin back."

"I'm going to the ladies' room." Caroline scooted back her chair and left.

Natalie smiled. Her friend always knew what was needed.

After a few beats, Chloe cleared her throat. "He gave me more information about Sherry."

Natalie frowned. Other than Sherry's prognosis, she didn't know what was actually wrong with her. "Oh? What did he say?"

"He said they found a tumor during her last mammogram and the biopsy came back malignant. The cancer has already spread to her lymph nodes and everything." Chloe looked up at her sister. "She probably doesn't have a lot of time, Martin said, since the cancer has spread to other organs as well."

Tears stung Natalie's eyes. She still felt anger toward Martin and Sherry, but her feelings were complicated now that Sherry was dying.

Chloe sighed. "I don't know what to feel. I still have so much anger, you know?"

"I do. Maybe we should talk to someone?"

"Who? Like a therapist?"

"Yeah."

"I don't know. Maybe." Chloe was silent. "You've got enough going on right now playing elf."

"True …" Natalie avoided her eyes.

Caroline walked up to the table and, having heard the last part, said, "I'm sure Mason can help you avoid whatever problem is occupying your life."

Natalie threw a whole blueberry muffin at her, hitting her in the face.

"Hey! It was just a suggestion …"

"It was a good suggestion." Chloe giggled wildly and dodged another muffin.

FIVE

Natalie looked up and groaned at the shining faces of expectant children and their impatient parents. Tugging at her red-and-white-striped tights, she closed her eyes and tried to hide the annoyance on her face.

Mason elbowed her in the ribs. "Elves are jolly, Natalie. You do *not* look jolly. You look constipated."

"I hate this job," she said through gritted teeth. "I look like an idiot!" She gestured at the green velvet dress that fell just above her knees.

Natalie would have looked silly if she were anywhere else. Her elvish shoes paired with the tights were ridiculous, and the bells on her wrists seemed cartoonish. Yet she looked stylish standing next to Santa Claus's red-and-gold chair at the mall.

"I'm right next to someone else who looks like an idiot—"

"Excuse me?" Mason interrupted.

She put her gloved hand on his shoulder. "I mean, you look great. For an elf."

Mason was the perfect elf with his dark-brown hair and a light dusting of freckles over his nose and cheeks.

Children eagerly weaved through the mall's North Pole on their way to visit Santa's Enchanted Forest, their eyes sparkling at the intricate decorations. Natalie tried to understand the reasoning behind the mall's commitment to the forest. After all, more adults bringing their children to see Santa meant more money spent in the stores, but that wasn't always the case.

"What's the point of all this? Half these people don't even stick around to shop. They come in, get free pictures of their kids with Santa, and hurry out of the mall," Natalie complained.

Mason smiled and waved at the children. "Natalie, have you ever thought they do it because they want it to be a special time of year for the community?"

She rolled her eyes. "Oh yeah, and Santa can actually visit every home in one night."

"He really can!" a little boy said, clapping his hands.

Natalie bit her tongue. As much as she hated Christmas and all its happy trappings, cynicism was not to be shared with the public, including the children.

"You are absolutely right," she said with her best elfish smile.

Mason handed him a candy cane. "Don't forget to keep an eye out for Santa on Christmas Eve."

Natalie dragged Mason behind Santa's chair. "Why do you encourage these kids?"

"What do you mean 'encourage?'"

"You fill their heads with nonsense. It's cruel to support these lies."

Mason's eyes grew flinty and his jaw hardened. "The world already has enough 'truth,' Natalie. Children aren't allowed to be children. Adults complain when children's movies aren't entertaining enough for the parents. Saturday morning cartoons are gone. Kids barely get recess."

Natalie glanced around. There were children everywhere, and they seemed happy.

"What does it matter if children get one holiday to believe in magic? It's *one holiday*! Let them have it and get over yourself, Natalie." Mason walked away to prepare for Santa's return.

Natalie crossed her arms and took a deep breath. Christmas was in a week, and she would never be an elf again. This was literally the worst job she had ever taken.

Silver bells rang, intermingling with the excited murmurs from the children.

"Ho, ho, ho!" Santa called out. "Happy Christmas, everybody!"

"Welcome back, Santa," Mason said cheerfully.

"Thank you, Mason! We're missing an elf. Where's Natalie?"

Natalie slipped into place. "I'm here, Santa. Sorry, I was just a little behind, thinking …"

Santa peered at her over his spectacles. "I see. Anything you want to talk about?"

His twinkling, kind eyes made her feel like he already knew what was troubling her.

"No, thank you. Especially not when we have all these children to talk to!" Her false enthusiasm stuck in her throat, and she began to cough.

Mason patted her back. "Are you okay?"

Natalie cleared her throat. "It's just a tickle. I'll be fine."

Santa looked at her and wrinkled his brow, genuine concern reflecting in his blue eyes. She had no idea where management had found this guy, but he came each year and refused to be paid.

Natalie turned to Mason. "Do you recognize anyone?"

Mason nodded toward the front of the line. "We've got the Thompsons, Johnsons, and Reynolds over there. And it looks like the Millers brought the grandparents for their annual family picture."

Her eyes widened. "How do you remember all these people?"

"I've been working with Santa for a while. Since high school?" He left it as a question, which was puzzling.

Natalie laughed. "You both have memories like cameras, I swear."

Mason looked at her, brows raised and mouth agape.

"What?"

"You laughed. You look nice when you laugh."

"Someone has to be the heavy around here," she teased. "Who's going to be Santa's bouncer if everyone's nice all the time?"

The line grew longer by the hour, but Santa only became more cheerful with each visitor. Natalie was losing her resolve to have more holiday spirit. Her cheeks hurt from smiling, and her throat was sore from fake-laughing.

The holiday spirit can just take a seat, Natalie decided. Being a grinch was easier.

"Natalie?" Mason carefully asked.

"What do you want?" she snapped.

"Can you get Santa more cookies? Only bring ones that aren't broken and *don't* eat any of them." He closed his eyes and paused. "I mean, it's no big deal if you do, but I don't think you'd like them. Er … I'm sure you'd like them. They're delicious! It's better if you don't because … because we only have enough for Santa," he stammered.

"Don't worry, I won't eat the freaking cookies."

Natalie stepped into the little cabin behind Santa's chair. Retrieving a plate, she grabbed the metal tin that was supposedly from Mrs. Claus. They received a new one filled with beautifully decorated sugar cookies each week. Icing delicately traced each one in lacy designs and edible glitter. She placed six of them on Santa's plate.

"Dang it!"

Natalie held half of a snowflake cookie while the other half rested on the plate. Broken cookies weren't allowed because they would ruin photographs. She quickly replaced it and was about to dump it into the trash when Mason's warning filled her mind: *Don't eat any of them!*

Stupid Mason. She wouldn't have thought about eating them if he'd kept his mouth shut, but now all she could think about was tasting it. Shoving it into her mouth, Natalie closed her eyes in appreciation. It was as delicious as it was beautiful. The buttery cookie melted in her mouth, the icing a perfect balance of sweetness.

Hurriedly wiping her hands and mouth, she looked in the mirror to see if she'd grown another head from eating the forbidden cookie and took the plate to Santa. He winked at her as if he knew, but that was impossible.

Mason immediately approached her. "Did you eat a cookie?"

Natalie laughed. "No, I didn't eat a cookie! Why are you so protective of them?" She laughed again, but her laugh didn't sound the same. Putting her hand over mouth, she looked around to see if anyone had noticed.

"You ate a cookie. Darn it, Natalie, I tell you not to do one thing …" He took off his cap and ran his fingers through his hair. "Maybe it won't be so bad if it was just one," he mumbled.

"You're worrying for nothing, Mason."

For the rest of the day, Natalie noticed each child's smile and giggle. She witnessed every parent who became teary-eyed when

Santa interacted with their child and remembered their names. For the first time, Natalie didn't feel annoyed or short-tempered.

When it was closing time, they said farewell to Santa, and security walked the elves to their cars.

"Be careful with what you say, Natalie," Mason warned.

"Why?"

"Because you ate a cookie. I know you did."

"What's going to happen, Mason? Is a gang of elves going to come and bust my kneecaps?"

He sighed. "Just … be careful. I'll see you tomorrow."

Natalie laughed. "It's not like I'm going to go around demanding the twelve gifts of Christmas or something. Goodnight."

Mason groaned. "Oh God … no …"

SIX

Natalie stretched and enjoyed the warmth of her bed, the dream fading from memory. The dancing sugarplums that had occupied her sleeping thoughts waved goodbye and giggled as they disappeared. Never before had her dreams been so vivid.

Working for Santa must be invading my dream space.

Slowly opening her eyes, the scene before her came into focus. Six bundles of feathers were neatly piled on top of nests on her bed, their long, elegant necks twisted under their wings. Natalie gasped, waking the geese next to her. She crawled backward on her bed as one waddled up to her—revealing a nest full of eggs—and honked in her face, only to waddle back and plop down onto her eggs.

Natalie slid from her bed and opened her bedroom door.

Chaos filled her living room. Ladies were dancing between leaping men, drummers were drumming, pipers were piping, and girls were milking cows on her back patio.

She shut the door and tip-toed past the geese. Grabbing her cell phone, she went into her bathroom and found swans swimming in the bathtub.

She called Caroline. "Get over here right now!"

"What is wrong? You sound like you have a zoo over there," Caroline said.

"Caroline! I have everything going on over here, get over here!" Natalie disconnected the call and stared at the swans. *What the heck is happening?*

She answered her phone when it vibrated in her hand.

"Mason! What the heck is going on?" she screeched. One of the swans honked in the background.

"You have swans, don't you?" he asked calmly.

"You know I have swans, dummy!"

"Have you found the French hens, the turtle dove, the—"

"*You* did this to punish me for the cookie, didn't you?" Natalie hollered.

"No, no, no! I told you to be careful, and you said something about the twelve gifts of Christmas! This is *your* fault!"

"You get over here right now and get rid of everything!" she demanded.

"I'll talk to Santa and see what I can do," he replied and hung up.

Oh great, he'll talk to Santa and see what he can do.

How had her life become so ridiculous?

This can't be real. This must be what insanity is like during the holidays.

Fifteen minutes later, Caroline walked into her bedroom. "What the heck are you wearing?"

"What do you mean? I'm wearing my pajamas," Natalie said.

"You have elf pajamas now?"

"Oh my– What *am* I wearing?" Natalie looked down at her long white nightgown with candy-striped ribbons woven into the lace. The tiny bells sewn onto the bows and embroidered candy canes were far too elvish to deny.

"Excuse me, Mistress," one of the leaping lords interrupted. "Your pear tree has arrived. I've put it on the patio."

"Oh, thank you," Natalie replied, then looked at Caroline. "What am I saying?" she whispered.

Caroline shrugged. "This is … wow. No words, Nat."

Mason walked in and looked around. "Wow, okay, this is worse than I thought. You not only ate a cookie but you also have awakened the Elf magic in you."

"Shut up, Mason." Natalie shot a glare his direction.

He held up his hands. "Hey, don't shoot the messenger and all that, right? I'm just telling you what Santa said."

"You are literally telling me I am an elf because I ate a cookie?" Natalie jabbed at his chest with each word. "That's insane."

"No, I'm saying you already *were* an elf and the cookie just made you more magical."

Caroline stared at both of them. "It might explain why you're so anti-Christmas, Natalie. Maybe something happened to make you the opposite of who you were supposed to be—"

A crash in the living room interrupted her.

"Can we take care of all of this," Natalie gestured wildly around her, "first? Then we can talk about that other stuff?"

Mason looked at the mess. "Oh yeah, definitely. All you have to do is say what you want to literally happen. But not *too* literally. It's a balance. If you are too literal, something like this happens." He pointed to the swans.

"Wait, so you're telling me I got the twelve gifts of Christmas because I was too literal?" Natalie looked skeptical.

"Well, yeah. You took the holidays and their meaning so literally that it was impossible for you to enjoy them. To you, if you thought Santa couldn't *literally* visit every home in one night, or if reindeer couldn't *literally* fly, there *literally* was no magic," Mason explained.

Understanding began to dawn on Natalie. "So I had to literally say something for it to literally come true for me to see the holidays aren't supposed to be like that?"

Mason smiled. "Exactly."

"Okay, so to get rid of everything, what do I need to do?"

Mason took her hand and led her over to the sleeping geese. Sitting next to her, he said, "I'm sure you know what you need to do."

"What? But I don't!"

He smiled. "You do."

Keeping her eyes closed, Natalie stretched and enjoyed the warmth of her bed. Mornings like these were her favorite, and luxuriating in the silence was something she treasured.

Wait.

Silence.

She hopped out of bed and ran to the living room where she found no dancing ladies or leaping men. There were no geese on her bed either. Her bathtub was empty.

Thank goodness.

Slipping back into bed, she thought back on the dream she'd had. It was vibrant and real, and it felt as if it had lasted hours. She drifted back to sleep for a while longer until she had no choice but to get up and go to work.

Natalie was uncharacteristically happy as she chatted with people in line for the Enchanted Forest and handed out candy canes to children. Her chest felt light, and she wasn't cranky. When she and Mason tied ribbons onto candy canes, she tied bows quickly and artistically.

"You're in a good mood," Mason mused as she made paper snowflakes.

"I know. I don't know why, nothing has changed."

"You ate a cookie; that's what changed."

She rolled her eyes. "Stop. What is it going to do, make me an elf?"

He barked out stilted laughter but paled. "Why would you ask that? Of course, it won't."

Natalie laughed but stopped when her dream came back to her. "I'm being careful with what I say, just like you told me."

"Good, I'm relieved."

"Yeah," she said slowly. "I'm trying not to be too literal. Or anything." She raised an eyebrow, waiting for his reaction.

His eyes grew wide, and he grabbed her elbow and pulled her behind Santa's chair. "All right, what do you remember?"

"What do you mean?"

"What do you remember from this morning?"

"It *wasn't* a dream! I had swans and geese and milking maids … Oh my God …" Natalie panicked as the pieces clicked together.

"Calm down. It's okay." Mason hugged her, patting her back.

"It's *not* okay, I'm turning into an elf!" she sobbed.

"Who's turning into an elf?" Santa interrupted.

"Oh God!" Natalie wailed.

"I'll take it from here, Mason," Santa said. "Let's go for a little stroll, Natalie." Santa offered his arm, waiting for her to wipe her eyes, and she took it.

They walked in silence for several minutes, Santa smiling at people and nodding at children who pointed him out to their parents. Finally, Natalie's hiccups faded.

"Why do you dislike Christmas so much, Natalie?"

She suddenly felt shy, as if having to tell a fine artist why she hated his masterpiece. "I … I just don't see the point in the holiday. Everyone always acts so happy and cheerful, but that's not the way they are all the time. Why have a holiday for something we should be like every day?" She glanced at him and could see he was honestly listening, so she continued.

"I don't think it's right to let kids believe in something so magical and beautiful as Christmas when we know magic and beauty don't truly exist. Why do we do that to them? It's like letting them believe they can fly only to let them fall from the sky on purpose. It's cruel," she whispered.

Santa looked concerned. "You don't think children should be permitted to have hopes, wishes, or dreams? Just *real* experiences?"

"How else are we to prepare them for real life?"

He was silent for several more minutes until they found themselves outside, standing in a patio. The night was clear, and Natalie could see every star against the dark sky.

"How old were you when you were adopted, Natalie?" Santa asked softly.

Natalie's jaw dropped. "How did you know?"

His eyes twinkled. "Let's just say I have a way of reading people."

Natalie turned away from the sky and looked at Santa. "I was six years old and had been in the orphanage for three years when they told me I was finally going to have a real family. I was so excited!" Her eyes dimmed. "But having a family wasn't that great, to be honest. It was nothing like they'd told me it would be."

"There are some homes Santa doesn't go to, whether it be for religious observations or cultural reasons. But Santa isn't allowed into some homes because the parents won't open the doors to him, like your parents."

"Yeah, we didn't celebrate any holiday. Not because of religion or culture, but because my sister and I weren't special enough to have holidays. I mean, I guess we weren't because my parents always forgot to celebrate them. The days would come and go like any other day. Chloe and I learned not to hope for Christmas or anticipate it. We just knew it wasn't happening. We didn't have birthdays, either," Natalie explained.

"You just had a lot of real-life experiences," Santa said.

Natalie stood there silently, his words hanging in the nighttime air. Were her life experiences the same ones *all* children should have?

"Ready to go back?" Santa gestured toward the entrance.

"I think so, but I have a question."

He laughed, "Are you an elf?"

"Well, Mason said—"

"I don't think you're ready for the answer, Natalie. Mason is worried about your reaction if you know the whole story." He looked at her over his glasses. "What do you think?"

"I woke up with geese on my bed this morning, Santa. I might need time to process things."

He held his belly and tossed his head back, "Ho, ho, ho! I think you're right." Pulling a small snow globe from his pocket, he handed it to her. "When you're ready to know the answer to that question, the globe will tell you."

Natalie peered at the object in her hand. "But there's nothing in it, Santa. It's just an empty globe."

He winked at her. "That's what you think."

They walked back to the Enchanted Forest, and Santa nodded at Mason, assuring him that everything was all right.

"You're worried for nothing, Mason, I'm fine." Natalie gave him a small smile.

"I just wanted to make sure."

She smiled. "I appreciate it, but I am. I feel great, and I'm being careful with what I say and not being too literal."

He looked visibly relieved. "That's super important. I mean, this is a really busy time of year, and I can't be running around cleaning up after French hens."

Natalie laughed and knelt down to talk to a little girl standing in front of her. "What can I do for you, sweetie?"

"What do *you* want for Christmas, Miss Elf?"

"That is so sweet! Well, you know ..." Natalie looked up at Mason and winked, "only a hippopotamus will do."

The little girl ran off, squealing in delight.

Mason groaned. "Oh God ... no ..."

SEVEN

"I said I was sorry, Mason. You don't have to glare at me like that." Natalie tucked the blanket and tarp around the squirming creature in the back of Mason's truck.

Mason stopped wrapping the blanket around the protesting lump and looked up at her. "I have a hippopotamus in the back of my truck, Natalie. I think I have a right to be a little upset right now."

She wisely kept quiet for a few moments and then dared to speak up. "But it's a really cute hippo ..." She trailed off.

He wasn't in the mood for the baby animals, it seemed. He'd warned her about being careful with what she said and she still said she wanted a hippopotamus. Natalie grimaced. Was she going to have to watch her words forever, or just until Christmas?

"Get in," Mason directed.

He turned to her after they hopped into the truck. "Look, I'm sorry I was grumpy. It's just ... I didn't think I would be smuggling a hippo into the zoo so close to Christmas." His eyes softened, and the mall's lights brightened the highlights in his hair. Natalie's stomach did a curious flip-flop, but she didn't want to think about it when there was a baby hippo in the back of his truck.

She looked down, breaking eye contact. "It's okay, Mason. You were right and I shouldn't have teased you by even saying I wanted one."

"What did you say? Did you say I was right?" he teased softly.

"Yeah, well, don't get used to it." Natalie laughed.

He turned his key and left the parking lot. "Still, I should have thought of how scared you might have been waking up to find a hippopotamus in your bathroom."

"Well, it wasn't necessarily worse than lords leaping through the living room." She laughed again.

Mason laughed but then became serious. "So what's our plan tonight? I can't get arrested, you know. Santa needs me."

Natalie pulled a slip of paper from her purse. "My friend manages the concessions department at the zoo and said she would meet us at the northwest gate to let us in. The zoo has been closed for a few hours, so it should be safe for us to bring in the hippo."

He turned on the radio but kept the volume low so they could talk comfortably. "Remember to not even sing along with anything," he warned. "It's better not to take our chances."

"Is it going to be like this forever, Mason?" She hoped not. She couldn't imagine having to be so literal with everything she said and not be able to joke with Chloe and Caroline about anything. The world just seemed so flat.

"I really don't know. We'll have to ask Santa, but we'll have to admit you ate a cookie." His brows furrowed. "I mean, he won't be angry. I haven't ever seen him angry. He'll just be," he paused and cleared his throat, "disappointed."

Her heart sank. "Disappointed?" She'd much rather he be angry.

They pulled up to the zoo's northwest gate and found Natalie's friend waiting for them, just like she'd promised. "Hey, guys! Pull around to the hippopotamus habitat and we'll unload it."

Mason slowly followed her through the zoo and parked in front of the enclosure. Natalie hopped out of the truck and gave her friend a quick hug.

"Thanks for helping us with this, Amanda."

"You bet. I mean, I don't know how you ended up with a hippopotamus, but we'll take it. You unload her, and I'll take her to the zoologist who stayed late tonight." Amanda went inside to alert the keeper that the hippo had arrived.

Mason started uncovering the hippo. "There you go, little girl. You'll be free soon enough."

"I've got something for her in my purse." Natalie reached into the truck, rummaged through her purse, and pulled out a Christmas bow. "Here it is!"

He smiled. "Looks like you're getting some of that Christmas spirit you love so much." He adjusted the bow around the hippo's neck. "There. You look beautiful, little hippo."

Natalie laughed. "I think she's smiling."

Amanda returned with the zoologist. "Hey, guys, thank you for bringing the hippo. What a great present for the zoo! How did you come across her?"

"Um ... uh," Natalie stammered, "it's kind of a long story, but I just sort of crossed paths with it."

"How do you cross paths with a hippo?"

Natalie panicked and looked at Mason. He ran his fingers through his hair and stammered, "Uh, funny story ... crossing paths. See, there was a path, and we were on it, and the hippo crossed it?"

Amanda, smiling the whole time, nodded her head and looked at them like they had been drinking. "Okay, well, I'm glad you did. I'll take over from here and give her a check-up. She'll be in quarantine for thirty days and then be out for the public to enjoy! Thanks again."

Mason handed over the hippo, and off she went to her new home.

"The zoo's Christmas lights are still on for another hour if you guys want to walk around while you're here." Amanda waved her arm around. "It's a small way to thank you for gifting us an entire hippopotamus. You can park your truck here and leave by the same gate."

Natalie nodded at Mason. "Let me just grab my coat."

They strolled past the lions prowling their enclosure, their cubs playing with red balls. Too busy pacing the artificial landscape lit with Christmas lights, the graceful cats were unimpressed by Mason and Natalie.

Natalie smiled at them. "They don't seem to care about much, do they?"

"No. Their whole life is right there. We don't matter to them."

Natalie watched the lioness groom one of the cubs, the baby impatiently trying to move away from the mother's enormous paw to continue playing in the grass. It was impossible; the mother tenaciously kept after the cub, her tongue lovingly stroking behind the cub's head until it was clean to her approval.

Natalie smiled. "Aww ... what a good mama."

The lioness released the cub, and it awkwardly ran away to catch up with its siblings.

Mason turned to Natalie. "Oh, I'm sure the mama is just following her instincts, don't you think?"

Her smile faded and her eyes went flat. "Not all mothers have that instinct. Let's go look at the monkeys." She quickly walked away from him, heading toward the monkey enclosure.

He raced after her and grabbed her arm. "Hey, I'm sorry. Did I say something wrong?"

She looked down where his hand met her arm and stared. He didn't move it, and she didn't pull away. His touch felt warm through her coat and it was the first time she noticed Mason didn't wear a coat even though there was snow on the ground. In fact, she'd *never* seen him wear a coat.

"No, it's just ... I don't know. Mason, I don't really have a mother. I have an adoptive mother, but she wasn't a mom." She let out a short bark of a laugh. "She was a 'Sherry'" Natalie looked up at him. "I don't know anything about a natural maternal instinct; I just know Sherry didn't have it."

Mason released her arm, and Natalie missed it. "Oh ... I should have been more considerate. I'm sorry."

"It's okay. You didn't know." Natalie reached out and touched his shoulder but suddenly felt awkward.

Silence.

Mason took her hand in his. "Well, we have about forty-five minutes left. How about we see what we can see and then take off?"

She smiled. "I'd like that."

EIGHT

Lying on her bed that night, Natalie turned the snow globe around in her hands, looking at its intricately carved wooden base and clear glass dome. Why would Santa give her an empty snow globe? The snow swirled around inside the glass, mesmerizing Nat and reminding her of the days she and Chloe sat in front of the large window in their childhood living room and watched the snow as it fell in circular whirls outside.

She shook the globe. The snow danced in the tumult she created until it settled around itself, and she stared at the emptiness inside once more.

There has to be a reason Santa would bestow such a gift, right?

Natalie laid back on her pillows and rested the trinket on her bent knees. The lamplight reflected off the glass in various directions as she gently moved it side to side. Running her fingers along the carved pine trees and reindeer on the base, she marveled at how something as simple as a snow globe could be so pretty— even if empty.

It was the first gift she'd ever been given.

Thinking about the lioness with her cubs and the conversation she'd had with Mason, Natalie sighed. "Why were Martin and Sherry so awful to us?"

The lamp's light filled the snow globe, as if it absorbed the illumination into its sphere. Natalie furrowed her brows and sat forward. "What the ...?"

Snow began swirling furiously within the dome, a mini blizzard contained in a small space, and the temperature dropped suddenly around her. Crawling beneath her covers to stay warm, Natalie kept her eyes on the magic unfolding in her hands. Beautiful, crystalline flakes, each individual in their shape and size, began falling around her as the temperature became comfortable yet still chilly. Regardless of the weather anomaly around her, the globe truly kept her attention.

The light within the glass dome began to dissipate just as the snow flurries slowed down. It was no longer empty but held a miniature replica of the home where she and Chloe had grown up. What's more, the scene appeared to be moving as she noticed a small car pull into the driveway. It was Martin and Sherry.

Natalie's eyes grew two sizes too big and she reached for her phone when Sherry exited the car. Keeping her sights on the scenes whirling before her, she tapped redial and spoke into the phone before the other person had a chance to say anything. "I need you to come over straight away. We need to talk." Hanging up, Natalie continued to watch the miniature tableau until its haunting end.

"What is this all about, Nat? I was in the middle of a streaming binge," Chloe said, walking into the living room and tossing her purse onto the couch. She turned to face her sister and put her hands on her hips. "The house is obviously not on fire. There aren't any sugarplums that I can see."

"Come with me." Natalie grabbed Chloe's arm and led her to her bedroom.

Taking a seat on one end of the bed, she gestured for her sister to sit on the other. The globe was between them, the snow still swirling.

"I already know you think I've been acting crazy lately with the whole the elf job, and because I told you about the swans showing up in my bathtub, but I need you to trust me with what I'm about to tell you, Chloe."

Chloe grew serious, her brows furrowing and eyes narrowing on Nat. "What's going on? Are you okay?"

"I don't know if *we* will be okay, but I need to tell you something." She reached over and took her sister's hands. "Martin and Sherry had a baby before they adopted us."

Chloe laughed, but she saw the pained look on her sister's face and stopped, growing serious. "What? Are you serious? They had a baby?"

"Yes. They had a baby boy and they were so happy! They weren't like they were with us." Natalie sighed. "It was so strange to see them young and happy …"

"But … how do you know this? How did you see them 'happy?'"

"The snow globe showed me."

Chloe's eyes grew wide and fill with mirth as she slowly pulled her hands away from her sister. "Your snow globe told you? The same empty snow globe the mall's Santa gave you? Come on, Natalie." She laughed nervously.

"I'm serious, Chloe. I was just lying here, wondering why Martin and Sherry were the way they were when it … came to life! Look, the snow in it is still floating around." Indeed, it was. The snow moved as if someone had blown it out of their hands, softly sifting it through the wind.

"We've been fidgeting and grabbed hands, Nat. Of course, it's moving."

"Well, maybe it will show you something. Hold it up and open your mind to the possibility, Chloe." Natalie held it out to her.

Chloe shook her head and sighed. "Okay, Nat. I'll try." She held it in the palms of her hands and softened her gaze, watching the softly rippling snow. The rolling drifts began to undulate in a circular rhythm, moving in such a way that Natalie thought her sister might fall into a trance.

Chloe gasped and leaned closer, her eyes focusing intently on the scene appearing before her. Natalie couldn't see what Chloe saw—the dome was filled with snow from her vantage point—but Chloe's eyes widened as she continued to watch the tiny images in the magic globe.

She set the globe on the bed, whatever secrets it revealed finally slipping away, and raised her head. "I—"

"You don't have to say anything." Nat placed her hand on Chloe's knee. "I couldn't find any words either. How could they never have told us?"

"The snow globe—" Chloe's words trailed off.

"I mean, I know we weren't the typical family, but to have a baby and not even mention it?" Natalie slipped off her bed and started pacing. "I feel … upset with them but also sad … I don't know how to process—"

"But it's magic and—"

Natalie put her hands on Chloe's face and turned it to face hers. "Snap out of it, Chloe. We need to talk about this!"

Chloe blinked a few times. "I'm … uh … I'm sorry, okay? You might be used to this whole 'magic of Christmas' thing," she said, making air quotations, "but I just watched little people come alive inside a glass snow globe, and that's kinda freaky, okay?"

Natalie kept her hands on her sister's cheeks and stared at her for a few seconds. "All right, I'll allow it."

"Thank you! Now get your hands off me." She pulled away from the grip.

Natalie let go and, wiping her hands on her hips, stepped back so she could look at Chloe. "You're really freaked out about this, aren't you?"

"Um, yeah! Things came alive inside that thing," she said, pointing at the trinket.

Natalie took it from the bed and placed it on her dresser. Sitting back on the bed, she faced her sister. "Okay, so what did you see?"

Chloe averted her eyes. "Same as, uh, you. Martin and Sherry."

Natalie waited for her to say more. When she didn't, Natalie prompted, "And the baby?"

Chloe looked confused and then matched her expression to Natalie's "Oh, and the baby, so sweet and young …?" She let the statement hang as a question.

"Are you sure that's what you saw?" Natalie's eyes narrowed.

"Yes! Yes, that's what I saw. Why? What did you see?"

"The same thing. And I can't believe they never told us, especially since it was so tragic that the baby died."

"Wha— Oh yeah, so tragic!" Chloe stammered.

Natalie furrowed her brows, not believing her. "Did you see anything else?"

"No. Nothing else. The baby died. So awful." Chloe raised her eyebrows and looked mournfully at her sister.

"Do you think this is why they adopted us?" Natalie wondered thoughtfully. "Maybe they thought new children would help them grieve better."

Chloe's attention snapped back from whatever lost world she was in. "What? You mean like *replacement children*?" Her eyes flashed with anger. "They could have gotten a dog instead and then we could have gone to *real* families! We couldn't *replace* a dead baby!"

"Chloe—"

"Stop. Just stop. This doesn't excuse how they treated us, Nat. Just because someone has a bit of tragedy in their life, doesn't mean they have permission to spread that tragedy to others in hopes it lessens theirs." Chloe's eyes filled with tears.

"I know, Chloe. I'm sorry. I just wonder—"

"Why they don't love us?"

"Yeah. I mean, who could *not* love us?" Nat gave her a sly smile.

Chloe winked at her. "I bet Mason can't resist loving you." She laughed at her sister's bright-red face. "Oh, come on, Nat. You know you have a crush on him."

Natalie threw a pillow at her. "I do not!" She laughed. "We did hold hands at the zoo tonight though."

Chloe caught the pillow and threw it back. "The zoo? What were you doing at the zoo?"

"We were delivering the baby hippo that showed up on my doorstep after I wished for one, and then we walked around the zoo." Natalie froze, knowing she'd said too much.

Chloe looked stunned. "A baby hippo? How on earth did a baby hippo just show up?"

"Nothing. Just forget I said anything."

NINE

The mall was quiet except for the Christmas music playing over the sound system. It had been closed for at least an hour, but the elves were busy in Santa's Enchanted Forest. It was two days before Christmas and a lot needed to be done.

Of course, the real Santa wasn't at the mall, and Natalie knew that, but she had slowly grown to love her experience as this Santa's elf. Sure, he might really think he was Santa, but that didn't do anyone any harm. Mason kept him out of trouble, and both of them did a lot of good for the community.

She blushed when she thought about Mason. Turning to see where he was, she spotted him sweeping the Peppermint Bridge and smiled. She lowered her eyes and fanned her fingers up at him shyly when he stopped what he was doing and waved at her. Frustrated at her inability to act normally around him all of a sudden, her cheeks grew hot.

Everything was fine until their date with the baby hippo made her have *feelings* for Mason, which would be fine if he had them too. But—

"Silly baby hippo," she muttered under her breath.

"You all right, Natalie? You seem lost in your thoughts tonight," Santa said.

Shaking her head, she went back to tying ribbons on candy canes. "Oh, I'm fine, Santa. I just have a lot of things on my mind." Unroll, tie, bow, snip. The monotonous rhythm of tying ribbons into bows on the candy helped her tonight, soothing the tumultuous thoughts of what she'd witnessed in her snow globe.

"Anything you want to talk about? I've been around a long time, so I can be a good listener."

"Oh, I don't ..." She paused.

Actually, talking to Santa might be helpful.

He wouldn't be around after Christmas, so she wouldn't have to keep talking about it. And he was not completely in the right mind, so he probably wouldn't remember anyway. She didn't have to be embarrassed by revealing her family's problems.

"Santa, I found out why my sister and I were adopted," she finally said after tying a few more bows.

He raised his white brows. "Oh, really? And what did you find out?"

She was relieved he made no mention of the snow globe. "Um, well, it appears Martin and Sherry—they're my adoptive parents—had a baby before they adopted me and Chloe. The baby didn't survive. I guess they thought we could replace him." She shrugged. "Chloe is really mad, but I don't know how to feel about it."

"Hmm ... I see. That would be quite confusing. How did you feel when you first found out? What was your first emotion?" Santa put his hands behind his back and looked at her.

"Confused, to be honest. At first, I wondered, how could they get over their first child and just ... get two more? But then I felt, wow, this must have been so devastating to experience, right?"

"I imagine it must have been. To lose a child would be heartbreaking, especially one that was wanted and loved."

Natalie paused. She hadn't really considered how they felt for this child when he was alive, only how they felt after he passed. She frowned. "Is it selfish of me not to have even thought about the baby in those terms?"

Santa looked confused. "In what terms? Being loved and wanted?"

"Yeah."

He paused a moment. "No. I think it's natural not to think of someone you don't know as being a full person who had been loved and cared for, let alone someone who has passed away. I *do* think it says you are beginning to find your answers now that you are thinking this way though."

"Maybe they adopted us because they thought they could love and care for other children like they did their first, but then they realized they couldn't. Maybe they hadn't grieved long enough?" Unroll, tie, bow, snip. Unroll, tie, bow, snip.

Santa took a candy cane before Natalie could wrap it with a bow. "I think you're reaching a point where you can start a conversation with Martin and Sherry." He unwrapped his candy and walked back to a grove of trees to fix some lights that had come untangled from the branches.

Natalie thought about what he said. *Could* she have a conversation with Martin and Sherry about this? Possibly. How would she explain she'd found out? She couldn't bring up the snow globe. She peeked up at Mason and smiled when she caught him watching her from Cocoa Canal.

Lost in thought, Natalie continued with the rest of the candy canes, completely focused on her task. She mindfully ignored the Christmas music playing around her —no more hippos!—until her humming naturally began to dip and flow with the tune around her. She didn't notice how loud she was until Mason called out to her.

"Natalie, stop!"

Natalie looked up at him, puzzled, until it dawned on her. She turned white.

"Ho! Ho! Ho-ooohh!" Santa's belly-full laugh was interrupted by a baby's coo, and Mason and Natalie looked at each other, horrified.

Natalie panicked. "Where did he go?"

"I don't know! Where was the last place you saw him?"

"He was fixing lights in Gumdrop Grove," she said.

They ran over to the grove and started looking for Santa, calling his name. They soon heard his cooing. "Oh, oh, oooh!"

"Oh no ... No. No. No ... This can't be happening," Mason muttered. "Not so close to Christmas Eve ..."

"Over there! Look!" Natalie pointed to a red squirming bundle under a tree.

They crept closer and found baby Santa, dressed in a red flannel jumpsuit with white fur cuffs and feet. He held a candy cane like a rattle, his red stocking cap over his eyes.

Natalie gasped. "Holy shi–"

Mason shoved her shoulder. "Not in front of the baby."

"Oh yeah, sorry. What was I humming? I didn't even notice! I'm so sorry. My mind has been so occupied tonight." Her voice waivered, nearly giving in to tears.

He shoved her again. "Can't you guess?"

She stared at the baby again, and the horrible realization fell on her. "Oh no. No. No. No …" She'd been humming "Santa Baby."

"Which 'Santa Baby' was it?"

Mason looked at her incredulously. "Which one? Why does it matter?"

"I don't know. I just wanted to know if it was Earth Kitt's or Taylor Swift's. I'm not thinking right, okay? I'm panicking!"

Mason grabbed her by the shoulders. "It was Ariana Grande's."

He put his head in his hands and paced back and forth. "What are we going to do? Santa's a baby? Christmas is in two days!" A feral look flashed in his eyes.

"I don't know. It's the mall's busiest day. Maybe we can get another Santa?"

He grabbed her by the shoulders and looked earnestly into her eyes. "I don't care about the mall; I care about Christmas! Christmas Eve is tomorrow! Who is going to deliver the presents?" He released her and started pacing again, muttering more to himself than Natalie. "There is no plan for this. I don't know what to do. We've got plans for weather and a broken sleigh, we know what to do if a kid catches us or—"

"Mason," Natalie quickly walked over to him, "calm down. I don't know what you're talking about, but I think you're near a breakdown. Breathe." She made him face her and they breathed together. "Good, keep breathing."

She walked over and picked up the baby Santa, wrapping him in the red-and-white blanket that was underneath him. Gently, she pried the candy cane out of his grip. He clapped his hands gleefully. "Oh! Oh! Ooh!"

"Come on, boys. We're going on a little bye-bye." She took Mason's hand and led him toward the door.

Once at Natalie's car, Mason said, "Where are we going?"

"Well, I don't know if they can help, but we're going there anyway. You hold the baby." She handed Santa off to Mason, who held him awkwardly.

Taking out her phone, Natalie called her sister. "I need you to meet me at Martin and Sherry's. We've got a situation."

TEN

N atalie pulled up to the house at the same time Chloe did.

"This better be a real situation, Nat," Chloe slammed her car door, "because you know I never wanted to come back here." She went silent when Mason got out of the car holding what appeared to be three- or four-month-old baby.

"I hope you've had a good night, sis, because I've been turning Santa into a baby during mine," Natalie replied.

"What the he–"

"Um, not in front of the baby, please," Mason interjected.

"Sorry, but what are you talking about?" Chloe looked confused.

Natalie sighed. "Okay, so here's the thing. I ate a magical cookie belonging to Santa that causes things to literally happen. So when I told you about 'The Twelve Days of Christmas,' they literally showed up in my house. So on and so forth. Tonight, without realizing it, I hummed along to 'Santa Baby' and this happened." She pointed to the bundle in Mason's arms. "Santa turned into that baby."

Chloe laughed hysterically. "Okay, sure. And Mason is really an elf, right?"

"Look, we don't have time to convince you this is real because tomorrow is Christmas Eve and I need Santa as an adult so he can deliver presents," Mason urged, rocking the baby.

Chloe laughed even harder. "I will play along because this is more fun than what I was doing at home."

"Chloe, just don't be difficult, okay? When we get in, go up to the attic and bring down the bassinet that's still up there." Natalie turned to walk up the sidewalk.

"Ugh, fine!"

After knocking on the door, Natalie, Chloe, and Mason stood on the front porch like the three wise men with their own baby. Soon enough, Martin opened the front door, his eyes widening.

"Oh, he-hello!"

"Hi, Martin, sorry to bother you." Natalie pushed her way inside, the rest following.

"Come on in," Martin said after they had all entered and shut the door. "Sherry, look who's here."

Chloe darted up the stairs and pulled open the door that led to the attic, disappearing inside.

"Oh my, hello." Sherry tried to stand from her chair.

Natalie was stunned by her appearance. She was gaunt and pale from the last time she had seen her, which was only a month before.

"Please, Sherry, don't get up. I'm sorry to interrupt your evening, it's just that I have a problem and I-I didn't know where else to go. It just felt natural to come here." Natalie reached over and took baby Santa from Mason, who went over and sat in an armchair out of the way.

"A baby?" Martin looked confused.

Natalie's heart softened at the pained expression on Sherry's face.

"I have a lot to tell you, and I know you won't believe me, but you need to hear all of it in order to understand the problem."

"Luckily," Chloe interrupted, dragging the bassinet into the room, "a sheet covered this, so there isn't so much dust." She stopped next to Natalie.

Sherry stifled a small sob. "How did you know that was up there, Chloe?"

"A magic snow globe told me."

"A magic …" Sherry's voice trailed off in confusion.

"I don't understand it either, but I can explain the snow globe," Natalie said. "But I have a few other things to explain first." It took several minutes, and she had to repeat her latest adventure with the baby hippo a couple times—only because Chloe enjoyed hearing about it so much—but everyone seemed to be more or less caught up, even if somewhat skeptical.

"Santa gave me an empty snow globe and told me it would give me my answers when I was ready for them. When I got home from taking the hippo to the zoo, I asked the globe why we were raised the way we were ..." The room filled with an awkward silence.

Natalie continued. "Anyway, the globe sort of came alive and started to show me scenes with both of you."

"Both of us?"

"Yes, you, Sherry, and a baby," Chloe interjected.

"Chloe ..." Natalie murmured.

"What? I'm just hurrying the story along."

Natalie cleared her throat and looked at Martin and Sherry. Tears ran down Sherry's cheeks, and Martin moved to hold her hand.

"Yes, I saw you with your baby. I'm sorry for your loss."

The room was silent for several minutes before Martin began to speak. "We had wanted a baby for so long. When we finally got pregnant, we thought we were the luckiest people in the world. Stephen was born and everything was perfect. *He* was perfect." He stopped, squeezing Sherry's hand. "People didn't know much about SIDS back then, you know? He was just gone ..."

"I know, and I'm sorry. We don't need to talk about it," Natalie said.

Chloe cleared her throat loudly.

Natalie glared at her. "At least not yet. We don't need to talk about it yet."

Sherry cleared her throat and wiped her eyes. "So are you going to tell us where this baby came from?" She couldn't take her eyes of the red flannel bundle.

Natalie leaned over and took the baby Santa and handed him over to Sherry. She awkwardly held him, as if not wanting to curl the wee one into her body at first, but soon she adjusted the baby so his head rested comfortably against the crook of her elbow as she wrapped her other arm around him.

Santa cooed, "Ho, ho, ooh!"

"Oh my." Sherry looked up, her eyes wide. "It sounds like he is trying to say 'Ho, ho ho.'"

"Yeah, that's because he is." Natalie bit her lip. "I accidentally hummed 'Santa Baby' tonight, and well …"

Martin laughed. "And you turned Santa into a baby?"

"Martin, this isn't funny!" Natalie flopped onto the couch.

Chloe sat next to her. "I told you it was funny."

Natalie threw her arms up in frustration. "We need to un-baby him, you guys! I need help! Mason is over here in the corner completely broken down." She gestured at Mason who was muttering to himself about contingency plans as he madly cut out snowflakes. "Mason! Why are you making snowflakes right now?"

"I don't know, Nat, it's just something I do when I'm stressed, okay?" She would never understand how he managed to always have crafting materials available whenever he needed them. Somehow, they seemed to just … appear.

Chloe held up an advent calendar she found on the coffee table. "Wait a minute, what the he–"

"Chloe, dear, not in front of the baby," Sherry admonished.

"Sorry. We never decorated for Christmas, or any holiday for that matter. But now that we're out of the house, you guys go crazy and get an advent calendar?" Her eyes narrowed. "Why didn't we ever get advent calendars?"

Martin suddenly looked uncomfortable. "The neighbor brought it over to us and said they were giving them away at the pharmacy."

She held it up and pointed at him with it. "But you kept it, and you're opening the doors each day. You're eating the chocolate!" Chloe stood. "Unbelievable, you guys. What else do you have hiding around here?" She went into the kitchen.

Martin started to stop her but gave up, looking at Natalie. "I mean, it's just an advent calendar."

"Yeah, but it's what that advent calendar represents, Martin. I'm disappointed," Natalie bit out.

He hung his head like a reprimanded child.

"I personally don't care if you have it. I just want to understand." Natalie looked at both of them, waiting for one of them to answer her.

"And I found a Christmas chocolate orange!" Chloe held it above her head.

"I-I wouldn't say it's necessarily a *C-Christmas* chocolate orange," Martin stammered. "Don't they sell those year round?"

"No, they don't." Chloe set it on top of the offending advent calendar and sat back down, crossing her arms.

"Help us understand, Martin," Natalie repeated.

He looked over at the sleeping baby Santa and his wife and sighed when she nodded. Sitting back down, he folded his hands as if in silent prayer and began to explain the unexplainable.

"After we lost the baby, Sherry fell into a terrible depression. We didn't understand she still had what we now know to be post-partum from the birth, but she did. Coupled with the profound grief from Stephen's loss, Sherry descended into an awful darkness that lasted for several years." He patted her hand as she shrank into her chair as if she still carried the shame of feeling depressed.

"I was getting a promotion at work that would benefit us financially, but I would be away from home for long hours. I was worried about leaving Sherry alone for long periods of time. We talked to our doctor about it, and he suggested we adopt a child, not as a way to replace Stephen, but as a way to move on with our family and look forward to the future.

"We put a lot of thought into it. There were long hours of discussion until we finally decided we would adopt. We would move forward. When we went to adopt Natalie, she wouldn't let go of Chloe at the orphanage, so we thought, 'Well, why not adopt both? That way they have each other.'

"Things went well at first. We were moving forward. I was able to leave for work and feel confident Sherry was doing well and you girls were thriving. And then the one-year anniversary of Stephen's death arrived and Sherry had a breakdown. You were too young to remember it, I think." Martin looked down.

"No, I think I remember Sherry going on a trip when we were really young," Natalie said. "To visit family?"

"Yes, that's what I told you, but really she went into the hospital."

If Natalie thought really hard, she could scrape up memories from before the time Sherry went away. She could remember a tea party in the back yard and playing dress-up in the bedroom. Chloe wouldn't remember any of this.

Martin continued. "Sherry wasn't the same when she returned. She had a palpable fear of losing you girls like we'd lost Stephen. It was a paranoia I couldn't convince her to break. Instead of continuing to bond with you, she distanced herself from you, not wanting to feel the grief of losing you again. And I, being the coward I was for so long, went along with it. I am so very sorry." He began to cry, silently at first and then openly sobbing. Sherry, too, had tears streaming down her cheeks and onto baby Santa's head.

Natalie reached over and gripped Chloe's hand. For so many years they'd felt unloved by their adoptive parents only to learn it was the opposite: Martin and Sherry were too afraid to love them.

Natalie stood and reached for Martin, hugging him for the first time she could remember. It was a warm and fulfilling hug, and it felt right. She went to Sherry and did the same, mindful of not squishing the baby.

Soon after the hugs, the miracle occurred.

ELEVEN

Nobody had noticed Mason for quite some time as it appeared he quietly soothed himself by making exquisite snowflakes in his chair off to the side. Yet even as he snipped and shaped, he followed the ebb and flow of the conversation, nodding in agreement at times or frowning at others. Santa was right all along, he always was.

Slowly, the pile of snowflakes—each as individual as a fingerprint—began to rise from their pile and swirl around above Mason's head. He paid them no heed. Continuing to shape the snowflake in his hand, he paused only to flick his wrist once to the right, which sent the snowflakes around the room with tinkling sounds.

Soon, the ceiling was covered with hanging paper snowflakes, tinkling together like tiny silver bells. Chloe was the first to notice.

"Look, Natalie!" She pointed at one hanging over her sister's head.

Natalie clapped her hands together in excitement. "Mason, what have you done?"

Sherry put down the baby Santa and held on to Martin's arm for support as she stood. "I don't understand. What's happening?"

Even tinier paper snowflakes began to fall from the larger ones, creating an illusion of a snowfall in the living room. It was truly magical, and Natalie held her arms to the side and turned slowly in a circle, her head tilted back and eyes closed. The snow fell around her, cascading over her face and hair. For a moment, she forgot about Santa being a baby and the sadness from her childhood. Right now, she just felt magic.

"Natalie, how is this happening?" Chloe held out her hands, catching tiny snowflakes in her cupped hands. "Mason? Did you do all this?"

Mason snapped his fingers, and his stack of paper and scissors disappeared. "I did. I told you I made snowflakes when I was anxious."

"But this … this is amazing …" Chloe's words drifted away.

"Sometimes, amazing things can come from difficult feelings." Mason shrugged.

"Girls," Sherry began, "I know we can never take back or repair the damage we caused you." Her tears started falling again. "But … couldn't we be a family now? I don't have much longer. I don't want to go knowing Martin is all alone, and …" Her voice broke.

Chloe's face softened at Sherry's words. Natalie nodded, and Chloe dropped her snowflakes, walked over to Sherry, and hugged her. "Neither of you are alone, Sherry."

The snow fell around Chloe and Sherry. Natalie watched was happy her sister had finally let go of her anger. She had, too, she realized.

"Oh, oh, ooh!" the baby cooed.

Everyone laughed as he played with the snowflakes falling in his face. Suddenly, they began to swirl in a circular pattern above his head. The tinkling sound grew louder, as if the bells had become impatient. Soon, the snowflakes gathered around the baby Santa and lifted him into the air, engulfing him in such a flurry that he could no longer be seen.

"Oh no, he's being eaten by the snow!" Natalie cried. "Mason, what do we do?"

"I-I don't know! I don't know! What are we going to do?" He pulled out a sheet of paper from nowhere.

"Don't make any more snowflakes!" Chloe shouted.

The swarm of snowflakes carried the baby into the middle of the room, at least it seemed like it did—nobody could see the baby anymore, after all. It began to shake and shimmy, the tinkling grew discordant, and Natalie hurried everyone behind the couch to hide, expecting an explosion.

Natalie quickly realized her fear was misplaced. Soon, one leg wrapped in red velvet with a white fur cuff and black boot stuck out, followed by a red velvety arm with a mitten on its hand. Once all the appendages were poking out of the white ball of snowflakes, Santa's head burst from the top, his cap a little crooked, but his jolly eyes sparkling nonetheless.

"Ho, ho, ho!" He shimmied out of the rest of the snowflakes, knocking them to the floor. "I'm glad we all got everything settled here. I was getting cramped in that tiny body!" Tossing back his head, he put his hands on his belly and laughed. "My goodness, it is hard to be a baby. Mason, make a note: All baby stockings get extra treats this year!"

"Yes, Santa." Mason pulled out a stenographer's pad and added it to what appeared to be a lengthy list. With a snap of his fingers, it disappeared.

Natalie narrowed her eyes at him. "I have so many questions."

"Yeah, I figured you would. We can talk after Christmas; I'll be busy the next few days."

Santa looked around the room. "Well, Natalie, do you still have a lot on your mind?"

"Uh … I do. I just watched you erupt from a white snowflake hive, so yeah, I have a lot on my mind." She crossed her arms and looked at her sister. Chloe stared at Santa, eyes wide and blank. Natalie sat her down and patted her shoulder.

"I don't know what just happened here, but I don't understand it. I don't believe it. I don't like it. And I don't even think I'm really here. I think this is all a hallucination. But I am taking the chocolate orange." Chloe crossed her arms and stared at everyone, daring them to contradict her.

"Well Chloe, we can't force you to believe," Santa said. "But I have a feeling you'll change your mind."

Martin put one hand on his hip and held out the other. "So you're telling me that not only is Santa real, but my daughter has been working with him for the past month?"

"Ho, ho, ho! That's right! She's been a good elf too! Now, this place needs some spirit. You can't celebrate Christmas with just an advent calendar and a Christmas chocolate orange!" Santa looked around the room and pointed to the corner, summoning a fully decorated Christmas tree. He conjured a garland on the mantel and wreathes on the sconces. Christmas mice hid in the houseplants and, finally, he placed poinsettias on the coffee tables. Snowflakes of varying sizes fell around the room and reflected off the lights of the Christmas tree.

He looked at Natalie and winked. "You know, my sister-in-law doesn't like poinsettias for some reason, but I think they make a room look cheerful."

"Wait a minute," Natalie said, her eyes growing wide. "If Victoria is your sister-in-law, that means she's …"

Santa winked again.

Sherry carefully walked over to Santa, visibly weakened from the whole experience, "Thank you, Santa. For everything." She looked up at him, her eyes full of tears, and placed her hand on his arm.

He gently patted her hand and led her to the sofa. "It was my pleasure, Sherry. Have a very merry Christmas." He smiled. "There is just one more thing," he said, his eyes twinkling.

Mason frowned and looked at his list. "What is that, Santa?"

He put his hands on his belly, threaded his fingers together, and rocked back and forth on his feet. "You and Natalie are standing underneath the mistletoe."

"Oh! Well, that's just a silly tradition. Mason doesn't need to actually follow through on that." Avoiding Mason's gaze, Natalie couldn't stop babbling; her words spilled like water and she knew it.

"Natalie." Mason stood in front of her and gently raised her chin. "Natalie," he repeated softly.

She melted at the look in his kind eyes. His snowflakes still fell, and it was like nobody else was around them. "Yeah?"

"We can't disappoint Santa, can we?" Mason smiled.

Natalie put her hands on his shoulders. "No, we shouldn't disappoint him at all."

His smile grew right before he lowered his head, softly touching his lips to hers, hesitantly at first. Natalie rose on her tiptoes to meet him halfway, greeting his kiss with a little sigh before tilting her head slightly. The kiss was warm, happy, and it made Natalie's heart skip a beat before running away in its rhythm entirely.

Finally, the sound of everyone clapping registered in their ears and they broke away. Natalie blushed a little when she noticed everyone staring but then she noticed all the snowflakes. It was like time had stood still for the snow as they kissed and every snowflake hung in midair. They began to fall once again before long.

Miracles have a way of bending even the smallest detail to their will.

TWELVE

The house was quiet, but her mind was not when Natalie walked in and hung up her jacket. Mason had dropped her off with another kiss, which she welcomed, but what would happen once he and Santa were finished with Christmas?

She frowned.

Was she ready to admit he was an elf and Santa was … Santa? Natalie sighed and put her hand inside her pocket to pull out the snowflakes she'd pilfered from Martin and Sherry's house. They weren't there. She tried to dig deeper, thinking maybe they had crumpled into a stitched corner, but there was nothing in her pocket. The snowflakes were simply gone.

She smiled.

It seems the magic was only for the moment and only while they were at the house. Natalie slowly walked over to her tree and gently touched the garland and ornaments. She'd never had a tree before this year. Mason had convinced her to get one and then brought over decorations he "happened" to have. Victoria was right; her heart did need lightening. The house looked more cheerful, even merry and bright. She took out her sketchpad and began drawing.

The McIntoshes had already had their Christmas party, but Natalie still owed Victoria a rendering.

Natalie woke up to the chime of her phone early Christmas Eve. Rolling over, she grabbed it and read the text.

> Chloe: What happened last night?! I am so confused!

Natalie laughed.

> Oh, you know, I turned Santa into a baby, Mason is an elf, and Santa turned back into an adult. Oh, and he's REAL! PS we forgave Martin and Sherry. Kinda a big night ...

> Chloe: Omg... this has been a heck of a week. I'm going back to bed ... btw if you marry Mason, will you live in the North Pole?"

Natalie rolled her eyes.

> Hardy har har

Tossing her phone to the other side of the bed, Natalie stared at her ceiling and groaned. Why did Chloe have to mention marriage? Married? To an elf? Is that a thing? Suddenly, the snow globe began to glow.

Natalie groaned again. "Oh no, what's next? Is a reindeer my uncle?"

She slid off her bed and grabbed the globe, the snow slowly churning in a circle just as it had before. Slipping back under her covers, her back propped up against the pillows, Natalie held it in front of her and waited for the scene to be revealed. Soon, the snow began to clear and the misty swirls gave way to a full moon reflecting off the snow and countless snow-covered pine trees standing upright in fields that surrounding at least one crystalline lake. Natalie couldn't differentiate the stars from the flakes and could swear she heard the sounds of a party.

Tiny voices carried through the night sky and over the lake. Soon, as if she were flying, the scene began to quickly span over the frozen lake and to a cheerful-looking building. It looked almost as if it were made of candy, but she knew that couldn't be possible—even if the snow collected on the eaves like frosting and Christmas lights as big as gumdrops ornamented the roof line.

The globe zoomed in on a window. Soon, the vision gave way to a Christmas party. No, a celebration party with everyone in costumes similar to what she wore at the Enchanted Forest.

Natalie gasped. *Elves. This is the North Pole.*

Elves made merry music with flutes and fiddles. One elf with bright-red stockings danced on a long workbench. Holding a large teddy bear, he fell into an enormous punch bowl. The other elves cheered as he hopped back out and carried on without missing a step.

More elves brought out enormous platters of cookies and cakes while others took away empty plates and glasses. Finally, Natalie saw one person she recognized: Santa.

"Ho, ho, ho!" she heard through the glass of the globe. "We have lots to celebrate, my friends!"

The elves cheered. It was clear this was a special night, one that was unusual in some way. Santa continued in his encouragement, talking about the record number of toys and games the elves had worked so hard to make, and how proud he was of all their endeavors. Natalie couldn't help but feel the same pride.

Wait, what is this? She peered closer at the scene before her.

Sneaking down the stairs was a tiny brown-haired girl who slipped into the next room.

"Aww … she wants to watch the grownups," Natalie whispered, a familiar pang in her heart.

The snow globe spun its point of view so she could see the little girl, her eyes wide as she watched the dancing and singing, hiding from everyone so she wouldn't get caught.

"Oh, but it's awfully late," Natalie said softly. "She should be in bed."

As if hearing Natalie's admonition, the little girl's eyes grew wider as she backed away from the doorway and looked behind her. Taking in the enormous sleigh with a large red velvet sack filled with toys and treats for the world's children, the child quietly tiptoed up the steps—obviously not wanting to wake the reindeer—and slipped underneath a fur blanket in the back seat. She soon fell asleep and the globe grew dark.

"Oh no, this can't be good." Natalie grew anxious. Santa would surely find her in time. There was no need to worry, right? She looked at the clock and swore. She was going to be late for the Enchanted Forest if she didn't hurry.

After rushing through a shower and donning her costume, Natalie slipped the globe into her purse at the last minute and rushed out the door.

THIRTEEN

Natalie burst through the doors of Northpointe Mall and was immediately greeted with a wave of anxiety. Last-minute shoppers walked blindly from one store to the next, the looks on their faces sending out signals of helplessness. Natalie dodged them and bolted for the Enchanted Forest. She was late and didn't want to disappoint Santa.

She made it through the crowd and to the elf entrance, pulling off her coat at the same time. Peeking over Santa's large ornate chair, she saw a line of excited children with their tense parents snaking their way through the forest. Natalie groaned. It would be a long day, yet she looked forward to it.

She slipped into place beside Mason. He reached over, squeezed her hand, and smiled. Natalie sighed with relief. She'd made it to her spot with seconds to spare *and* she felt excited.

Santa greeted each child by name, much to the delight of parents, and listened patiently to what each little visitor had to say. Natalie smiled and laughed, made babies smile for the camera, and handed out candy canes. Mason helped move the line along smoothly and chatted with those who waited, and Natalie realized she truly meant it when she wished everyone a merry Christmas.

"You seem happy, Nat," Mason said. "It's really nice to see some sparkle in your eyes."

Natalie shyly looked down. "Well, I guess I just realized that all of this," she gestured around her, "isn't just for kids. Adults are allowed to believe in some magic too. I guess I decided it was time for me to start believing."

"I think that is exactly what you needed all along." He winked at her and went back to work.

When it was time for their break, Natalie grabbed Mason by the elbow and led him over to Santa's cabin. "Mason," she hissed, looking around her to make sure nobody could hear them talking.

He looked over his shoulder and leaned in, his eyebrows raised. "What?"

"I need to show you something, something I don't understand."

"Um, okay. Do we need to still whisper?"

She rolled her eyes and pulled out her snow globe. "As you know, Santa gave this to me when I first started here." Mason took it from her and looked at it carefully, turning it over in his hands. Natalie lifted her eyebrows and lowered her head, whispering again, "And it's magic."

Clarity dawned in Mason's eyes, finally understanding what she was trying to tell him. "Oh, you're wondering how it works."

"Well, duh. I mean, Santa said it would give me answers when I was ready, and you know this is how I found out about Martin and Sherry's baby. It was pretty freaky at first, let me tell you." She snorted and lowered her voice again. "But it showed me something different this morning."

"What did it show you?"

"Well, I was texting with Chloe, and she mentioned mar—" Her cheeks heated when she remembered the conversation. "We were talking about elves," she finished. "The globe lit up and started doing its swirling snow thing, and the next thing I knew, it was showing me an elf celebration at the North Pole." She frowned, wondering if she should tell him the rest. "And it also showed a little girl who hid in Santa's sleigh."

He raised his eyebrows. "It ... it showed you that, huh? Um ... well, wow!" he stammered.

Natalie narrowed her eyes. She knew that look. It meant he knew something and didn't want to tell her. "What do you think it means, Ma-son?" She pointedly emphasized each syllable of his name, and he looked away nervously.

He fidgeted with his collar. "I ... I ... uh, I really wouldn't know. I think if you were talking about elves that it just decided to show you elves, unless you were talking about something specific, like, you were worried about elves in some way?"

It was Natalie's turn to look uncomfortable. Hurriedly, she replied, "No. Not all. No concerns, no worries. Elves are just … elves!"

"Yeah, just elves. No big deal. Elves." Mason cleared his throat.

Natalie pointed over her shoulder, "We, uh, should get back to work."

"Right."

"Right."

Santa stood in the Reindeer Ravine welcoming visitors when Natalie approached him. "Hello, Natalie! Merry Christmas!"

"Merry Christmas, Santa." She looked around and smiled. She would miss working in the Enchanted Forest.

"Something tells me you have some questions for me." He looked at her, a bushy white eyebrow raised high. "Maybe they have something to do with your snow globe?"

Natalie sighed. She should have known he would know. "I do, Santa. It has shown me some things, and …"

"And you want to know how it works?"

She nodded.

"I suppose just telling you it's magic won't be enough?"

She shook her head.

He laughed deeply. "Let's have a seat over on this bench, Natalie."

He led her to a park bench that was ordinarily meant for mothers and their babies. Instead, Santa and Natalie sat together while she held her snow globe with two hands in front of her.

He pointed at the globe, and the snow began to swirl. "That snow globe was made in my workshop by two elves. They wanted to create something that held enough of their individual magic that the person who held it, the person who was meant to own it, would be able to spin the magic as if it were their own and use it to reveal answers to their questions."

The globe lit up as Santa spoke, lighting the internal flakes as if they were crystals, creating prisms beaming from the center. The snow swirled and swirled, a tumult of winter firmly contained within the glass ball.

"But I don't understand. Why can *I* see my answers then?"

Santa pointed to the globe. "Watch."

She raised the globe to eye level, and the scene slowly unfurled before her. The little girl, still hidden underneath the furs of Santa's sleigh, had fallen asleep. Santa hadn't noticed her when he'd hefted himself onboard, and off he flew with a tiny stowaway in the back seat.

Natalie watched him land his sleigh in front of the St. Mary Margaret orphanage and hoist his enormous sack over his shoulder, entering the building through the door Sister Catherine held open for him.

Sister Catherine didn't notice the door had gotten stuck on a snow drift and didn't close all the way. And neither did she notice the newly awakened little girl scamper off the sleigh and slip into the orphanage.

"St. Mary Margaret ..." Natalie looked up at Santa. "That was my orphanage ..."

"Yes, I know, Natalie." His eyes were kind and gentle, but they were filled with remorse, too, for not having noticed she was in the sleigh and then leaving her behind.

"But—"

"We looked frantically for you back at the Pole, not realizing you were left at the orphanage. I'm so sorry, Natalie." His eyes filled with tears, and Natalie could see how the years of sorrow and guilt had weighed on Santa. Santa—someone so jolly and filled with joy—was also capable of feeling the very depths of heartbreak. This was what love truly was: radiating light even in the darkness.

She gently put her hand on Santa's cheek. "I forgive you. You didn't know what happened. It's not your fault I wandered away from the Pole."

Santa took out his handkerchief and wiped his eyes, cleaning his spectacles before he put it away. "I have come to this mall every year because I knew there would be a time we would meet and I could give your snow globe to you."

Natalie paled at the realization. "Does that mean my real parents are ... elves?"

"It does. You're an elf, Natalie."

Everything felt heavy and the world began to go dark, and Santa grabbed Natalie before she fell to the floor.

FOURTEEN

Natalie blinked against the bright lights and tried to focus on Santa and Mason as they loomed over her. She looked around and realized she was lying on her couch with a blanket covering her.

"Welcome back, Natalie! We were getting worried." His kind eyes peered over his spectacles as if he really did know everything.

She grimaced a little as she tried to sit up and felt the rising panic from the truth come over her again. "I don't understand. How can I be an elf? I am not little. I don't have pointy ears ..."

"Hey!" Mason interjected. "Those are all stereotypes against elves." He began to pace the room. "We look like normal people, you know. We're just uncannily good with crafts and art projects."

Natalie thought back to her childhood when she'd made a kite and it had turned into a dragon. She held her head in her hands. "How can this be possible?" she mumbled. "How am I going to tell Chloe? Or Martin and Sherry? Oh my God, am I going to have to live in the North Pole?"

Mason sat next to her. "No, you don't have to live in the North Pole. I don't live there. And you can tell your family the truth ... or not, or wait until you're ready. Nothing has to happen right now." He smiled. "Everything is going to be okay."

Natalie looked at Santa. "But what about my parents? I mean, my *real* parents?" *Do they want me?* That was the real question.

Santa knew what she was really asking though; he always knew. "They've never stopped wanting to see you, Natalie. Once you were adopted and had a life here, they didn't want to intervene. But they knew you'd come looking for them when you were ready."

Natalie released her breath in a *whoosh*. "I want to meet them. I just don't know if I'm ready yet."

The thought had never crossed her mind to look for her birth parents. Now she knew who and where they were, but she didn't know how she felt. Natalie dropped her head into her hands.

"When you are ready, all you have to do is open the door," Santa said.

She lifted her head. Santa held out a brass key about the size of a business envelope, and she took it from him and turned it over in her hands.

"Open the door?".

Santa pulled out another brass key. "Yes, open the door. Watch …" He walked to her coat closet and touched the doorknob with the key. When it glowed a golden yellow, he turned the knob and opened the door.

Natalie gasped at what was beyond the threshold. Snow flurries rushed into her living room, and she was greeted with a night so dark, its only illumination came from a bright full moon with its accompanying stars. But what held her attention most was the cobblestone path that led to a workshop a short distance away where she could just barely hear music and revelry drifting across the winter wind.

"The North Pole is … in my closet?" she whispered.

Santa laughed. "It is wherever your heart leads and beyond any door you wish to open. As long as you have a key," he added with a wink. He schooled his features and spoke gently, "Your parents will be happy to see you whenever you're ready."

She clutched the key to her heart. "Thank you, Santa."

"Natalie, I hate to leave you now, but I need to go." Mason looked worriedly at her. "Can I call you when I get back from, well, you know …"

Natalie looked from Mason to Santa, who was trying hard to pretend he wasn't paying attention. "Oh yes! Yes, of course. You have a … a job to do!"

"I'll be back for Christmas morning, Natalie." Mason stepped close and pulled her in for a kiss.

Leaning back to see him smiling at her, Natalie winked. "And I'll be dreaming of a—"

He playfully pinched her lips shut. "Don't."

She laughed.

Mason followed Santa across the threshold, and as the door shut behind them, paper snowflakes began to fall from Natalie's ceiling, large flakes at first and then smaller, more intricately designed ones. She held out her hands and caught them, smiling and then laughing as they swirled around her, covering her tree and tickling her nose.

Natalie called Chloe, and her sister picked up on the first ring. "Merry Christmas, Chloe."

Her sister was silent for a moment and then answered with a smile in her voice. "Merry Christmas, Nat. We're a pair of festive elves, aren't we?"

Natalie snorted. "You have no idea."

"What do you mean by that?"

"Nothing," Natalie said innocently.

"Nat? Seriously, what does that mean?" Chloe's voice rose with panic.

"I'll see you tomorrow, Chloe." Natalie smiled.

"Nat, I mean it, if you're—"

Natalie didn't hear the rest of whatever Chloe was saying because she disconnected the call. She held the phone in her hand and hesitated for a minute before finally texting a short message to Martin.

> Have a very merry Christmas! If you and Sherry would like, I can stop by tomorrow for a little while...

She held her breath and tapped send, suddenly feeling like a child again waiting for Martin to come home from work and hoping he would notice her. Natalie let out her breath when a text flashed onto her screen.

> We would love that. Feel free to bring Mason too.

Natalie settled back onto the couch and pulled the blanket back up to her chin, not caring she was still in her elf uniform. It wasn't really a uniform anymore, was it? Drifting off to sleep as the snowflakes continued to fall around her, magically melting into the carpet in spite of them being made of paper, Natalie felt serenely happy.

She had everything she needed—on *both* sides of the door.

ABOUT THE AUTHOR

After writing and illustrating her first bestseller in second grade, "The Lovely Unicorn", C. Streetlights took twenty years to decide if she wanted to continue writing. In the time known as growing up, she became a mother, poet, and badass. Retired from teaching, C. Streetlights now lives with her family in the mountains along with their dog that eats Kleenex. She published her first memoir, *Tea and Madness*, in 2015. *Black Sheep, Rising* was selected as a 2017 Kindle Book Award Semi-finalist.

C. Streetlights is represented by Lisa Hagan Books.

CONNECT WITH ME:

Website:
www.cstreetlights.com

Twitter:
www.twitter.com/cstreetlights

Pinterest:
www.pinterest.com/cstreetlights

Facebook:
www.facebook.com/
CStreetlightsAuthor

Instagram:
www.instagram.com/
cstreetlights

Goodreads:
www.goodreads.com/
cstreetlights

BookBub:
https://www.bookbub.com/
authors/c-streetlights

Amazon Author:
www.amazon.com/author/
cstreetlights

LinkedIn:
www.linkedin.com/cstreetlights

Newsletter sign-up: